DATE DUE

W9-AJT-701

AUG   6 2002

MAR 2 6 2003

SEP 29 '04

DEC 27 '04

FEB 03 '06

APR 27 '06

NOV 2 9 '06

JUL   1 '08

JUL 2 4 '08

JUN 1 8 '09

NOV 3 0 '09

JUL   0 8 2010

JAN 2 5 2011

MAY 3 0 2011

WITHDRAWN

A NOTE TO PARENTS

Your public library is a friendly and fascinating place that can help you instill in your child a love of books and learning long before he or she is able to read. In fact, libraries today welcome babies and toddlers and offer more than simply books for children of all ages. Many have parenting programs to help you develop language skills and early learning concepts in very young children. For preschoolers there are story hours, records, films, and other events. And, of course, there are books, books, and more books—to read in the library or to borrow for home use.

By establishing a weekly library habit with your children from the earliest age, you are giving them a magical gift. Children who grow up feeling at home in the library will continue going to the library when they are old enough to use it alone. They will know that there is always another book to read or another event to enjoy. And that's a gift that will last a lifetime.

—Marguerite A. Dodson
Coordinator, Children's Services
Brooklyn Public Library

A VISIT TO THE SESAME STREET LIBRARY

A Random House PICTUREBACK®

A VISIT TO THE

Copyright © 1986 Children's Television Workshop. Sesame Street MUPPETS © Muppets, Inc. 1986. All rights reserved under International and Pan-American Copyright Conventions. ® Sesame Street and the Sesame Street sign are trademarks and service marks of the Children's Television Workshop. Published in the United States by Random House, Inc., New York, and simultaneously in Canada by Random House of Canada Limited, Toronto, in conjunction with the Children's Television Workshop.

Library of Congress Cataloging-in-Publication Data: Hautzig, Deborah. A visit to the Sesame Street library. SUMMARY: Grover shows Big Bird the many things to be enjoyed and the surprising services at the public library. [1. Libraries—Fiction. 2. Puppets—Fiction] I. Henson, Jim. II. Mathieu, Joseph, ill. III. Sesame Street (Television program) IV. Title. PZ7.H2888Vj 1986 [E] 85-18312 ISBN: 0-394-87744-6 (trade); 0-394-97744-0 (lib. bdg.)
Manufactured in the United States of America 1 2 3 4 5 6 7 8 9 0

SESAME STREET LIBRARY

by Deborah Hautzig • illustrated by Joe Mathieu

FEATURING JIM HENSON'S SESAME STREET MUPPETS

Random House / Children's Television Workshop

Big Bird was so excited! He had received five dollars for his birthday in a card from Granny Bird that said, "Buy something you will enjoy for a long time." And that was exactly what he was doing— buying books.

"There is nothing like a good book," he said. "And books last forever."

Soon he had found three wonderful books—two little storybooks and a great big book called *All About Birds*. He took them to Mrs. Hirsch, the bookstore owner.

"*All About Birds* is my favorite," Big Bird told her. Then he gave her his five dollars.

j38467

"I'm sorry, Big Bird," Mrs. Hirsch said, "but you don't have enough money to buy this big book."

Big Bird was disappointed.

But Mrs. Hirsch had a good idea. "I'll bet the library has *All About Birds*. The library has more books than any bookstore. And you can *borrow* them for *free!*"

"Wow, that sounds great!" said Big Bird. So he paid for the two little books and set off for the library.

When Big Bird got there, he saw some kids going into the big brick building. "I'll just follow them," he said.

The kids led him to a big, bright, busy room filled with shelf after shelf of children's books.

"Gee, Mrs. Hirsch was right," Big Bird said. "I've never seen so many books in one place!"

Then he noticed a woman with a hand puppet. The puppet wore a red cape and was talking to a group of children!

"Hey, that's Little Red Riding Hood!" Big Bird said.

"... and Little Red Riding Hood and her grandma lived happily ever after," said the woman with the puppet. All the children clapped, and Big Bird did too. "If you liked this story, you will also like 'Goldilocks and the Three Bears.' We have lots of fairy tale books," the storyteller said.

"Oh, I know where they are!" said a voice that Big Bird knew. It was Grover!

"Hi, Grover!" whispered Big Bird. "I never knew people read stories out loud in a library. I thought you had to be very quiet."

"Oh, no," said Grover. "I come to Mrs. Libby's story hour every week. She's the librarian. Sometimes we even put on little plays. Last week I was Little Boy Blue! Would you like to come with me next week?"

"Sure!" said Big Bird. "But right now I am looking for a special book called *All About Birds.* There are so many books here! How do you find the one you want?"

Grover said, "Do not worry. I, Grover the Finder, will show you!"

Big Bird followed Grover. Everywhere Big Bird looked he saw something interesting.

"Look at that poster!" said Big Bird.

"I borrowed it twice," said Grover.

Big Bird was amazed. "You can borrow *posters,* too?"

"Sure," said Grover. "And I will show you something else you can borrow."

They came to a sign that said LISTENING CORNER. Grover pointed to boxes of all kinds of records and tapes.

"You can borrow records and tapes to take home and play," Grover said. "Or you can listen to them here."

"You can?" said Big Bird happily.

LISTENING CORNER

"Yes," said Grover. "That's what these kids are doing."

"But why are they wearing earmuffs? It's not cold," said Big Bird.

Grover laughed. "Those are not earmuffs! Those are headphones. When you use them, only you can hear the music. Pick a record and I will show you."

They looked at lots of records. There was even a section called Talking Records. "These are like story hour—somebody reads a story on a record," Grover explained.

Big Bird picked *Peter and the Wolf,* and Grover put it on for him. In a minute Big Bird began shouting, "Hey, everybody! This record has talking *and* music!"

As they left the Listening Corner, Big Bird saw a girl carrying a bright orange paper duck.

"That's pretty," said Big Bird. "Are you borrowing it?"

"No, I am keeping it. I made it!" the girl told him. "You can make one too. A lady from Japan is teaching everyone how to fold paper into all kinds of things. It's called origami."

"This month is the Japanese Festival," Grover explained. "Come on, let's go to the crafts table."

Big Bird and Grover had a wonderful time. Grover made a blue sailboat and Big Bird made a pelican.

"Grover, this pelican reminds me of the book that I still want to find—*All About Birds*," Big Bird said.

So Grover took Big Bird to the bookshelves. Many of them had signs: TALES OF MAGIC; DINOSAURS; NOT TOO EASY, NOT TOO HARD.

By the time they got to the shelf of bird books, both Grover and Big Bird were balancing a stack of books they wanted to look at.

"I think there are more bird books here than there are birds!" said Big Bird happily as he added six more books to his stack.

"Let's take these to the Cozy Corner," said Grover.

"What's the Cozy Corner?" asked Big Bird.

Grover showed
Big Bird the coziest
corner he had ever seen.
Instead of chairs there
were big, soft pillows on the
carpet. It was the perfect place
for reading. They joined the
other kids who were curled up with
books and magazines.

After a while Big Bird sighed. "These
bird books are wonderful, but they're not
All About Birds."

Grover said, "I will ask Mrs. Libby to help
us. She will know where to look."

As they left the Cozy Corner, Big Bird began putting books that he did not want to borrow on the shelves.

"Oh, no, do not do that," said Grover. "The library people put books back exactly where they belong so they will be easy to find."

Then Big Bird saw a man wheeling a cart of books and putting them back, one by one, in their right places on the shelves.

Grover and Big Bird found Mrs. Libby near some shelves filled not with books, but with toys!

"Our toy collection is something we just added to the library last month," Mrs. Libby proudly told Big Bird.

Big Bird thought it was wonderful. He picked up a bright red truck from the top shelf and gave it to a little boy who couldn't reach it.

"Say thank you to the nice big bird," said the little boy's mother.

"Maybe you can help *me*, Big Bird," said Mrs. Libby. "Our big map of the world is coming loose from the wall, and I am not tall enough to tack it back up."

"Can you borrow maps, too?" Big Bird asked as he tacked the map back up.

"No. Lots of kids use the maps and the books in this reference section after school to do their homework. So everything here has to stay here," Mrs. Libby explained.

"Boy, there's so much to do at the library, I almost forgot what I wanted to ask you. Can you help me find the book *All About Birds*?"

"Did you look on the shelf of bird books?" asked Mrs. Libby.

"Yes," said Big Bird. "But I didn't see it."

"I'll help you find it. I know we have that book," she said.

"Oh, good," said Big Bird. "I was afraid you might not have it."

"Even if this library doesn't have a book you want, we can probably get it for you from some other library," said Mrs. Libby.

"*Libraries* borrow books too?" said Grover.

Mrs. Libby took Big Bird and Grover to the shelf of bird books. She pulled a big book off the shelf and handed it to Big Bird. "Is this the book you want?"

It was exactly like the book in the bookstore. "Yes!" said Big Bird happily. "Gee, thanks! It was right here all the time, but I didn't see it."

"Once a book I wanted had been checked out by somebody else," said Grover, "so Mrs. Libby sent me a postcard when it was returned."

Big Bird liked the idea of getting a postcard from the library, but he was happy that *All About Birds* was there for him to borrow right now.

"I'm glad you got the book you wanted, Big Bird," said Mrs. Libby. "The library has something for everyone—even Braille books for people who cannot see."

Then Grover told them about the library on wheels that he used when he visited his cousins in the country. "They live too far from a library, so the library comes to them. It is called a bookmobile."

It was time to go. Big Bird and Grover had the books, records, and posters they wanted to borrow.

"Now you need a library card," said Grover. "When I got my library card, Mommy wrote a note for me to give to the librarian. It had my name and address on it. Do you have something that shows where you live?"

Big Bird looked worried. Then he remembered the birthday card that Granny Bird had sent him. He pulled it from his bookstore bag of books. On the envelope was written "Deliver to Big Bird, The Nest, Sesame Street." "This shows where I live!" said Big Bird happily.

"That's fine," said Mrs. Libby. Then she typed his name and address on a card. All Big Bird had to do was sign his name.

"Take good care of all the things you check out of the library," said Mrs. Libby. "Other people will want to borrow them after you."

"Oh, I will!" said Big Bird. "I promise."

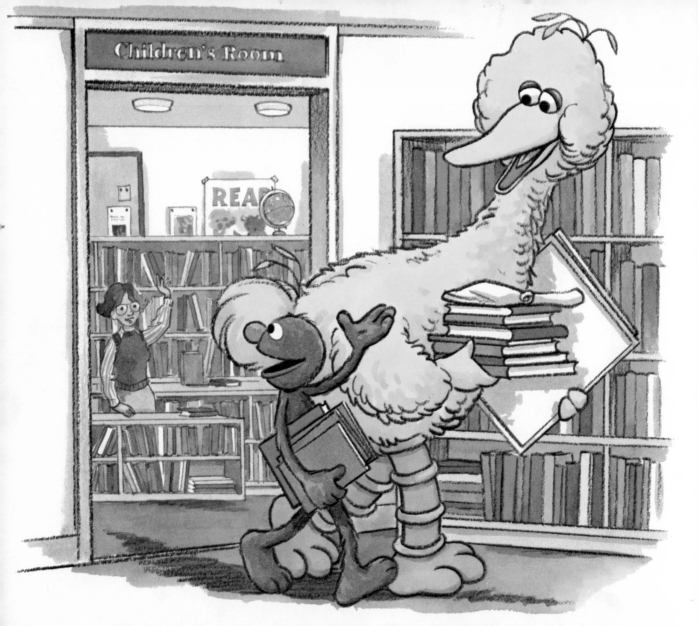

"Come back soon," said Mrs. Libby. "There's going to be a movie on Friday that you would like. It's about penguins."

"A movie," said Big Bird. "I'll be back all right. After I read *All About Birds*, I'm going to read all about everything!"